All the Way Up
IT BEGINS NOW

Published By
Rhea Leto Media Group, LLC
6854 Orcutt Avenue
Long Beach, California 90805
Phone: 424.250.3773
Email: rhea@rhealeto.com
www.rhealeto.com

Cover and Interior Design by
Rhea Leto Media Group, LLC
www.RheaLeto.com

ISBN: 978-1-947185-07-4

All the Way Up
IT BEGINS NOW

WRITTEN BY

Kevin Moreno
Adriana Romero
Abe Blancas
Joshua Toscano
Michael Blancas
Jeffrey Carrasco
Emely Toscano
Janette Lopez

RHEA LETO MEDIA GROUP, LLC

TABLE OF CONTENTS

Foreword

I grew up in Los Angeles, and I can't remember ever having the opportunity to become a published student author. I grew up in what is now known as South Los Angeles, and I've been an officer for seventeen years. As a Community Safety Partnership Officer, or CSP Officer, I'm exposed to many programs, but I'd never heard of a "resident dedicated" student author book publishing program, until now. These students stayed the course in spite of heavy workloads from school, personal challenges, and sometimes plain ol' writer's block. Their stories are insightful, encouraging, and powerful. When I was a child, I had mentors and father figures in my life. Although I didn't know it at the time, those individuals were sealing my future by making sure that I had the tools to be successful in whatever field of work I decided to pursue. They did this by constantly encouraging me, challenging me, and holding me accountable.

The PHABB5 program is one of the only programs I know of that allows youth to use the arts to control both their academic and professional narratives. I see so much of myself in the youth that I serve, and I'm always at a loss for words when I meet middle school or high school students ready to give up on themselves and life because of a bad circumstance or situation. That's why I'm challenging you to find a way to get a copy of *All the Way Up: It Begins Now* into the hands of at least one student in need of inspiration.

- Officer Olea

Doctors Get Sick Too
Kevin Moreno

"Dr. Michael Stevens! We need you in room 135! There's a young man who needs attending!"

It's 2:30 in the morning, and the ER lobby seems to be emptying. At first glance, it seems calm and relaxed. But behind the scenes, we have a patient who is rapidly dying. I can hear him screaming. He's shouting so loudly, I can feel my ears pop. My mind automatically averts its attention to the automatic sliding glass doors.

Two LAPD officers blow by me pushing a man who looks gang affiliated. He has six white bandages on his chest and stomach, shallow pools of blood forming in each of their centers. I raise my cup, the smell of French vanilla coffee filling my nose, but after so many hours the stuff starts to taste like water. I interlock my hands behind my back. A young Latino mother chases her toddler down the hallway. Out of nowhere a female voice erupts through the overhead speakers.

Every day is different down in the LA County Hospital, whether it's a stab victim or someone who just has a bad stomach flu. I've been living in LA since I was born. I graduated in 2009 with a doctorate in general surgery from USC. I didn't come from a wealthy family, but I committed to my studies and graduated from medical school. With my degree, I could have gone into an operating room. That's typical, but only in certain circumstances. When the higher-ranked doctors need someone who is more precise, they call on me. I like to believe they do it because they don't want me to take their job.

"Dr. Stevens, Dr. Stevens, are you even listening to me?!" My mind flashes back to reality. Dr. Stetson, my colleague and girlfriend, is hurrying me into a patient's room. As we rush down the hall, Dr. Stetson calls out, "The patient is a young male, and he has a bullet lodged in his left side under his throat." As we hurriedly walk into the room, I advise her, "Grab me some swabs, the scalpel, the suction tube, and the rest." I and the other doctors clean up the patient. I adjust the light to focus on where I make the small incision. The scalpel slits cleanly into the skin and then *POOF*.

Time seems to slow down and voices sound distorted. A soul comes up from the patient and says, "I'm no ordinary patient. I am this body's spirit. As you experienced, time has slowed down. I have pulled you from your own body to speak with you. You may be able to move, but you cannot go back without my command."

I start to struggle, panicking, as I have no control of what I'm doing.

Once again he speaks, but this time more weakly, "I have seen death before, and I've escaped many times. But now I must go. I can only tell you so much, so I came here to tell you that you need to be strong. I feel that you have greatness in you."

I go back to my real body, and I hear the flatlining of the monitor. I instruct a nurse to charge the defibrillator. As it begins to hum, we rub the paddles against each other. We discharge them on the body three times, but no response. He is gone. Another patient is dead.

I walk back towards my office trying to get the scene out of my head. I take a sip of coffee, and shake my head. I go back to my computer to look at the following times for patients who are waiting. My mind goes blank as I have a small trip. I feel dizzy, and everything seems to be spiraling. I fight it off and go back to my work. I do my normal rounds, examining patients' files, diagnosing, prescribing, until it hits five a.m. I finally head towards home in my Cadillac and lie in my bed. A few minutes later, I'm out like a light.

A few days later I receive a notice of temporary release. It reads, "DR. MICHAEL STEVENS. THIS LETTER IS TO INFORM YOU THAT AS A RESULT OF YOUR ACTIONS THESE PAST THREE MONTHS, YOU HAVE BEEN IS-SUED A SUSPENSION FOR TWO WEEKS." Having no idea for the reason of the notice, I go on to investigate. After a couple of hours scavenging for answers, I realize that it is because of the patient. He was the seventy-eighth patient that I've lost in the course of three months. I shake my head, rub-bing my forehead, thinking about how I'm going to get out of this mess.

I hear a knock at the door and tiredly say, "Come in."

It's Dr. Stetson. Not making eye contact, she says, "Hey Mike are we still going to—" She notices me on the verge of a breakdown. "Hey, hey c'mon, Mike. What's wrong?" She sees the release. "It's not that bad. You're thirty-six, you have a stable job, and plus it's only temporary. You'll get your job back in a few weeks."

It's infuriating. She doesn't understand. She doesn't know what losing control of your life feels like. The anger is form-ing like hot lava, rushing and rushing up until I explode. "Do you think I care about what you say or do? Huh? You know nothing. Okay? You, Diana Stetson, you know NOTHING. You're worthless! Absolutely worthless!"

Dr. Stetson leaves my sight, but before she leaves, she notes, "You may think I'm worthless, but I know you're gonna come back to me. And when you do, I won't take you back."

I hear about a meeting downtown about a new technology. This new technology is going to be able to improve surgical accuracy. I put on my suit, and my finest watch in the cabinet. I hop in my car and turn on the ignition. I'm going down the fastest route possible, and then there's a detour.

I ask the construction man, "What's going on? I have a meeting, and I'm gonna be late!"

Grudgingly, he answers, "We have construction work, sir. There's gonna be blockage for the next two hours or so. I suggest you turn around and find another way."

I type the address into my GPS—2785 7th Street, Suite #421. It shows me a route that leads towards a cliff. As I'm driving down the road, it begins to rain hard. Cars turn into blurs of light. As I check the time, a big rig appears in front of me. I try to swerve and nearly miss the truck. I'm not able to gain control of the car and swerve out. I hit the side of the cliff, bouncing me off of the road. I begin to fall. The windshield breaks and pieces are flying everywhere. Time seems to slow down, and I realize I have a split second to make a choice. I can either jump out of my car and save myself, or I can die and crash with my car and my life's work. My time's up. I'm too late. I over-thought it, and now I'm going to die. My car crashes, and I'm gone.

I wake up to a blinding light above me. I try to move, but it's no use. I hear a voice. It's Diana. She's crying and crying, and then she sees me try to get up.

"Mike! Oh, thank goodness, you're all right!"

I look at my hands. I try to move them, but it's no use. I look at the rest of my body in a panic. My whole body is in a cast.

I scream, "What happened to me? Why am I like this? Who did this to me?"

Diana calms herself down and uneasily says, "You got into a car accident. We found you on the side of the cliff. When the paramedics arrived your body was crushed by your car. The connections to your nerves were cut off. This was the best the doctors could do. There was no way that they could have fixed you." As she weeps, I realize that she is right. Nobody could've fixed me, even if it was for their life. I am going to live a life of no control. I'll slow down and become a burden to those who care and support me. I was once a person who had everything, but because of one selfish action, here I am.

I look at Diana, and she looks at me. Somehow we seem to be thinking the same thing. How did I get into this mess? I think about what the future has in store for me. Without realizing it I've been thinking aloud.

Diana says, "Everything is going to be ok. We'll go through your therapy sessions together. Then, after that, we'll get you back into the operating rooms. And from there, we'll see what the future has in store for us."

She smiles. Somehow that makes me feel a whole lot better. I take her advice and close my eyes.

Ten years later, I'm back on my feet. I realize that life is not about controlling, but about what you do to succeed. Through working miracles, I was able to move my limbs in two months or so. Although I'm out and about in my wheelchair, I'm still living through life day by day. After my accident, I became a mentor for future doctors, surgeons, and psychiatrists. I married Dr. Diana Stetson, and we have a big house. But even though I paint this picture to sound great, it sure has its ups and downs. Diana still has to look over me constantly just in case anything happens to me, and in case I need help grabbing my food or if I need to get up and go to the bathroom. Life has turned around since my accident. I would like to say that I regret my selfishness, but in a way, I feel that it was right. It was a sign that told me that it's not about me, it's about what I can do to get other people's lives in control.

Kevin Moreno

Life Is a Struggle
Adriana Romero

It was 4:20 in the afternoon. I was on my way to a sesh. As soon as I opened the door, I felt someone tap my shoulder. I turned around, and my mom was behind me with tears running down her cheeks.

I asked what happened, and she said, "Your dad left."

I acted like I didn't care, but I felt like a piece of my heart just died. I really didn't care, because he was never home. He was always out drinking. It hurt my mom, so it didn't matter to her that he left. She was fine, and no one really cared. When I left, I saw him outside. I went to go tell him to watch out.

Later that night one of the big homies called me and said, "It's done."

When I got home, it was 11:30. My mom was sleeping on the couch waiting for me. I took off my shoes and ran slowly to my room. I guess she heard me, because she came up a minute later and asked, "Where is your dad? He hasn't come back for his stuff."

"Throw them away or sell them. He's not coming no more."

At 6:00 in the morning, I woke up. I checked out the window to see if it was going to be a rainy day, but it looked nice like usual. As soon as I finished getting ready, I walked down to eat. There were tamales that my sister, mom, and I had made last night. As soon as I reached for my phone, my mom yelled, "Its 7:10. What time are you leaving?"

As soon as she stopped yelling, I ran out the door before she could come down.

As I walked down through the park, I noticed the old veteran wasn't at the park any more. I wondered what happened to him; I had no clue. When I hit the black step, I heard the train coming, and I ran the red light to catch the metro. When I got to the door, I noticed my wallet had fallen. I swore and started to kick the door, banging it with my hands. The bus driver opened it for me, but as soon as I stepped out, he closed the door and left. I started to walk. I had no other choice, because I was running late.

I got to school, and the teacher said, "The principal wants to talk to you."

I put my stuff down and went to the administration office. When I walked in there, everyone was quiet and staring at the devices in front of them.

I walked into the principal's office and said, "What now?"

She looked up and said, "I can't have you coming in late anymore. You're out."

I walked away and said, "Okay."

When I walked out of the office, I started wondering what I was going to do now. How was I going to tell my mom that I was getting kicked out again? My mom might send me to boot camp or put me in military school. I decided I was just going to wait until she found out. It'd take a while, since she couldn't really speak English.

Suddenly the bell rang for fifth period. As I walked back, I could hear gossiping around me. When I got to my locker, I grabbed my books and left for my classroom. As I walked over to my seat, I noticed the teacher staring at me.

When I sat down, she said "Finally you show up. You got a lot to do."

I laughed and said, "I know that for sure."

She handed me some work and told me, "You have until Friday."

I looked up and said, "Alright."

I waited for her to leave and started using my phone,

but decided to do some work because I wasn't doing anything else. I was having a hard time, but I understood somewhat. The bell rang and we went to P.E. class. When I walked into the gym they were doing yoga, and I just sat outside. I didn't think a little running could hurt, so I started a few laps around the field. When I was running, I saw the principal stand on the side of the field waiting for me.

Deep inside I was thinking, What does she want now?

As soon as I arrived, she said, "Stop. Go change. You're coming with me."

I walked over to the lockers. As soon as I got there, I started changing.

When I came out, she said, "Let's go to my office."

As I was walking with her, she was trying to talk to me about where I had been, and that all they were doing was trying to help me.

"Why don't you do what you're supposed to do? It's not that hard. We can help you," she said.

"Okay, how do you want to help me? By sending me to another school or putting me in programs I don't want to be in? Tell me how you're going to help me."

She said, "You have no choice."

Later that day I was thinking, Why not take the easy way

out and get some of my friends to do my work? I'm going to do that now. I just have to find a way to get money.

The bell rang, and I went for my stuff and left.

I walked over to catch the metro home.

When I got off the metro, I decided to hit up one of my homies.

I called him and said, "It's time."

I had to do some side jobs. It was starting to go good. I was thinking, why not reach the top like I always wanted? I had no other choice but to fight the streets. Little by little, people started respecting me, and I enjoyed it. I met more and more people, which meant business was going good. I started going to the big streets. I wasn't going to let anyone hold me back.

I went to my new corner. As usual, business was running. After four hours, I was about to leave, but my homies came through to congratulate me for starting my business alone. Twenty minutes later, a cop turned the corner and started walking towards me. I slowly started walking away.

He yelled, "Stop!"

As soon as I heard him yell, I ran through a little alley where my friend lived and threw my bag over his wall along with my phone and wallet. When I reached the light, I ran across and two cops pulled up in front of me. They pointed their guns at me and said, "Freeze!"

As soon as I stopped, the first thought that came to my head was of my Nino and my mom, because they practically raised me. When they handcuffed me, some really nice memories were going through my head. Tears started running down my face.

They dropped me to the ground with a knee in my back and said, "Smile, just like you were when you were running."

They took me and called my mom to tell her what happened. We arrived at the station, and they put me in a cell with other people. After a long while of waiting, my mom walked in and started crying.

I looked at her and my eyes got watery, but I didn't cry. I just put my hands through the cell and told her, "I love you. I am sorry. It's not your fault."

She hugged me for about ten seconds before the security guard pulled her away and said, "no touching."

She let go and said, "I am getting you out."

I gave her a kiss goodbye and told her, "Don't blame yourself."

A little while later my homie came through and told me I was only going to be in there for two days, because they hadn't found anything on me. I asked why, and he said he had seen everything happen, and when I threw the bag, he had gone to his back porch and got everything.

So, I wouldn't get caught. I thought, now I know who's got my back. I told him thanks and gave him a quick hug. Before he left, he told me to hang in there. I told him, "You know me, hanging until I fall," and he left.

After a long while, they started yelling, "It's time for bed." But a lot of people didn't want to sleep. I slipped in a crowded corner next to a buff guy because he looked scary, so no one got near him. They woke us up and wet us with cold water. They gave us a meal and left. I only drank the water and ate the Jell-O and went back to the little corner next to the buff guy.

I sat there until they said it was time for bed again. When they turned off the lights, the buff guy next to me asked me, "When are you out of here?"

I said, "Tomorrow, hopefully."

He asked, "What did you do?"

I told him my story, and he said, "I did something similar, but I had a gun on me, so they arrested me."

"How long are you going to be in here?" I asked.

He said, "Longer than you, that's for sure."

I said, "Goodnight. Nice talking to you," smiled, and turned my head.

He turned around and said, "Goodnight to you to."

They woke me up early and told me it was time to go home already. I went out, and my mom was waiting for me outside.

She said, "Why do you always do what you're not supposed to do?"

With tears running down my face, I just hugged her and said, "I love you."

"You got lucky this time. Next time, there might not be a next time. Okay, let's go."

As we were going home, she was yelling at me and telling me, "I hope you stop doing what you're doing, because you're the only thing I got left."

When I asked her why, she said my Nino had passed away. When she said that, I broke down and started crying in front of my mom. I was trying to calm down and asked her what happened. She said that he was scared I was going to jail. When we got home, I ran upstairs, got some clothes, and went into the restroom. I sat on the floor for ten minutes, got up, and went into the shower. Thirty minutes later, I was ready to go out with my homie.

paused. "Your mother is looking for you. We got a letter. She found out you're here."

I groaned. Ever since I was young, I never liked my mother or my father. After they told me about my mom, I went outside. I thought to myself, "Should I leave? What about my friends?"

I did not want to go back with my parents, so I told Mike and Derek, "I think I should leave."

They said it was the right thing to do. I remembered the bad times I had with my parents. The only people I actually liked were my friends. I decided to just leave.

That is how it started. I did not want to deal with it again. It was cold, but I didn't care. I just ran. I had to hide. This wouldn't be easy. I had not run from my parents since I had left their place years before.

I decided to hide behind a house. It looked empty. I camped there, then I feel asleep.

I woke up the next morning to a text noise on my phone. It was Mike. He told me, "Dude, the cops came 'cause ur mother told them about u." I read on. "They were questioning us. We stayed quiet." I was glad they didn't say anything. But then I read again: THE COPS. Oh no. Now I had to run away from both my parents and the cops. This was going to

She said, "Let's go stack up."

I told her, "Nah, actually, I don't want to go. I'm going back home already. My bad." When I was walking back home, the only thought I had in my head was, *Why did he leave when I needed him the most?* I started to realize people actually cared about me. When I got home, I looked at my mom, and ran to my room. I threw myself on my bed and said to myself, "It feels good being where you want, but there are always consequences."

Adriana Romero

Run
Abe Blancas

It all started when I was throwing bottles at the back of a bar. I didn't know what else to do at the moment. After a while, it got really boring and cold. It gets really cold down here in Detroit. My name is Vance, and I'm seventeen. I usually get judged just because I am black. I don't really mind. I hate cops and my parents. As long as I don't think about them, I'm fine.

I went back home where I lived with Mike and Derek.

Derek walked up to me. "Where have you been this whole time?" he asked.

"The usual. Throwing bottles, popping tires," I replied.

"Of course, you always like to do that," he said.

I managed a smile. He was playing with me. I could tel

It got real serious after that though. Derek looked at kinda funny, but then Mike walked in.

"Hey, you're not gonna be happy about this, but—'

be very hard. I thought for a second. I realized that in order to escape I had to keep moving, so I did.

I ran for about two hours, and then I stopped. I felt my heart skip a beat.

Up ahead I saw a gas station. I was relieved, because I was thirsty. Lucky for me, I had cash on me, so I decided to buy something. I did not want to waste too much time standing there. As I was buying something, I saw a cop car pull up. I felt myself freeze. I had to snap out of it, so I ran out as fast as I could. I saw him holding a piece of paper. It was a picture of me. I had no time. I had to run. He was going into the store. He was going to ask the cashier if I had been in the store, or if he had seen me. All of these things were running through my mind. I don't actually remember what I did for the last five minutes. I just knew that I was running.

Then, I stopped. I lost signed of everything. I was wondering, Should I just stop running? Should I just give up on everything I have just done? No. But I couldn't come to a decision. Should I go back? I thought to myself. "NO!" I screamed.

I was sweating. I couldn't handle all the pressure. It went quiet—no cars, no noise, nothing. I finally thought, I should just keep on going. I saw cop cars, so I hid behind a trash can.

Then I got another text. It was Mike again. "Your father, he di—"

My phone died off. I did not need to read more. After that, I felt my stomach drop. My father had just died. I threw up after that. What if he killed himself because of me?

After that, things didn't get any better. I just got more tired as I ran and avoided more cops. It wasn't as easy as it sounded, just hiding from them. I had been running from the cops and my mom for three days. I never wanted to go back with her. Every day after school, she would hit me for no reason. That was when I used to love to go to school.

I must have been thinking for a long time, because a woman walked up and spoke to me. She asked, "Hey, excuse me, are you lost? Do you need help?"

"No," I replied.

"Have I seen you somewhere before?"

I looked at her. I knew she recognized me. I had seen missing posters about me around town.

She walked away. I was thankful. I never really trusted women. Maybe that is why I didn't like my mother.

I saw the woman grab her phone, but I was gone by the time she could call the cops. As I was walking by a street lamp, I saw a cop car. I was scared, shaking, nervous. I decided to run. The chase was on. Two cops were chasing me. I looked behind, and they were far back. I made a right and hid in a bush. I ducked through one of them. I saw an empty building and went inside.

I could have just stopped and turn myself in, but I didn't want to. I closed all the doors, and it was pitch black. Five rooms were on the first floor, and four on the second. Two exits were at the bottom and top. Three if you counted the windows. I heard the cops, and I saw their flashlights. I was going to get caught. I remembered I had my phone. I threw it out a window, and they followed the noise. I ran out the exit, but I hit someone. I gave the guy one punch. I could have escaped then, but the other cops came. I got caught.

I was in the cop car, wondering what would happen to me eventually. I arrived at the station. My mom wasn't there though. I waited for about half an hour, and she walked in. I did not even remember what she looked like. She looked happy, but inside was a different story. She was an evil person. I did not want to go back with her.

I realized that I actually was not scared of my mom. I thought, "Why should I be scared of her?"

Brother
Joshua Toscano

I tried to keep my eyes clamped shut, but clearly this California Saturday sun had other plans. I woke up covered in sweat. I looked at my twenty-dollar fan and rolled my eyes. I sat on the edge of my bed, brushed sleep boogers out of my eyes with the backs of my knuckles, and then quietly opened my door. The first thing that I saw was my mom and brother getting ready to go to the doctor for a checkup. My brother had a cough that wouldn't go away. I wanted to be a doctor, someday, or maybe an engineer, or even an NFL player. I walked past the living room and made myself a bowl of cereal.

After breakfast I headed back to my room, but not before shouting, "It's Saturday!"

I slammed my door and started thinking about Stanford Middle School and all my friends.

After hours of playing games on my laptop, my mom walked in my room. Her face looked broken in a sad way.

"Jacob—" she said, clearing her throat. .

"What's wrong, Mom?"

"Your brother, Thomas—" She paused again, "he has can-cer." She walked over to me, sat on my bed and wrapped her arms around me. I pulled back from her. I was still trying to make sense of what she had just said. I stood up.

"Wait, wha—? What do you mean? Where?"

"It's in his lungs" she said.

As soon as I heard that, I felt like I was going to have a heart attack.

"He's at the hospital now. I can take you there, so you can see him." We got in my mom's red Honda Civic. She jammed her key in the ignition and sped out of the driveway. When we got to the hospital, we slammed the car doors and ran in, looking for my brother. On my way to his room, I almost bumped into a short Latino American man in glasses who was my brother's doctor.

"Oops, I'm sorry."

I introduced myself as Jacob, Thomas's brother. The doctor told me with a deep voice that he had cancer in his lungs, and there was a 66% chance that he would die. They were going to take him in for surgery the next day, but it would cost us a lot more money than we had.

When I heard that, I knew right away that I had to do something about it. My first thought was to get a job, but I remembered that I was too young, and no job would accept an eleven-year old kid. It would also mean that I would have to drop out of school, something I swore I would never do. I marked that off the list.

I sat with my brother for several hours. My mom left me there, so I could have more time with him. When I walked into my house later, sad, I realized that it was 9:30 p.m. I tip-toed to my room as quietly as I could. I could hear my mom snoring. It was late, and I sat on my bed thinking about how first I had lost my father, and now I might lose my brother. I could feel tears rushing to my eyes. I buried my face in my pillow and began crying.

I went to sleep, and in the morning, I went to buy break-fast for me and my mom.

When I was walking to the store, I couldn't believe my eyes. There, on the side of the road, I found a suitcase. I opened it, and it was filled with what looked like millions of dollars! As soon as I saw that money, my heart jumped with joy. I ran to my house with the suitcase, thinking to myself, Whoever left that large, black suitcase with money, I thank them a million times. When I showed it to my mom, I saw the excitement in her face. It was priceless.

She told me, "Jacob, with all this money, we can afford the surgery for your brother."

I said, "Yes, we can afford the surgery. And whatever else we want!"

I was so excited. Later, I turned on my Apple TV and put on TVBC news. There was a report about the case. Apparently, it had been stolen, and the police were trying to find it.

When I heard that, I told mom, "Mom, we have to return it."

"What about your brother?" she asked.

"Mom, we'll figure out a way. This would be stealing, and it's not right."

"Okay," she said reluctantly. My mom and I walked to the police station. She waited for me outside, while I brought the case in. As soon as the officers saw the case, they were shocked.

"What are you doing with this?" asked one of the tall police officers. Apparently, the case belonged to an old rich lady. I explained how I had found it but was returning it because I'd seen the report on the news. The lady who owned the case was sitting with the police officers.

"Wow, you're very generous, kiddo," she said as she took

the case from me. "You have really demonstrated that you're a great person."

"Yeah, it's what I do best. Well, nice meeting you."

I walked away, but my heart was sad, because I didn't know what we would do for my brother now. As I was crossing the street to get back to where my mom was waiting for me, I heard the old lady saying, "Wait!"

"Yes, ma'am?"

"What was the first thing you thought of when you saw all this money?" she asked.

"I thought, 'I'll be able to pay for my brother's surgery,'" I said. "He has cancer."

She opened the case, pulled out several stacks of money, handed them to me, and said, "Here, you need it more than I do."

"Oh no, no, it's fine," I said.

"Don't hesitate. Keep it."

Without thinking twice, I gave her a big hug and took the money. I ran back to my mom and showed her the money. We exchanged hugs too. I didn't know how much money it was, but every dollar mattered for my brother.

After breakfast we went to the hospital. When we got there, we entered my brother's room. My mom said that she'd stay in the room with him while I talked to the doctor. I said, "Okay."

I found my brother's doctor and asked him, "How is my brother?"

He said, "He was lucky that he came in early. We were able to take out the cancer. He will be out in two days."

I told my mom the great news, and she looked like the happiest mom in the world. After those two days passed, my brother came home, and we were all happy. I told him my brother all about the old woman and her gift of money. That seemed to cheer him up as he recovered.

He hugged me and said, "Thank you." I smiled.

A week passed, but for me it seemed like it was only a few days. Then the bill came from the hospital. It was a total of $256,794. We paid with the money from the old woman and still had a lot left over. The next day when I went to school. I realized it was the last day of the year. When I got my grades, I passed every class. I was going to high school! Plus, my mom was studying to become a doctor, and my brother would try out to be an NFL player after his recovery.

A few years passed by. I graduated high school and went to engineering classes. I became a lawyer, my mom became a doctor, and my brother became an NFL player. We became wealthy people and had a huge mansion. It was everything I had ever dreamed of. I had always known I was going to be very successful in life.

Joshua Toscano

Team
Michael Blancas

It was about ten p.m. and Christian was lying in his bed thinking of how the weekend was over and how he would have to return to school the next day. Although he didn't like school, he excelled in every class. Everyone considered him the "teacher's pet."

"Christian!" yelled his mother. "Come help do some chores."

If there was one thing Christian didn't like to do it was help or do things that he didn't find interesting. Quickly, Christian came up with an excuse.

"Can't right now. I'm studying."

With a firm tone, Christian's mother said, "Alright, but hurry up. You've got school tomorrow, and you have a tendency to come late."

With that, Christian turned off his lights, tucked himself in, and was ready for what he thought was going to be a normal day the following morning.

When Christian walked into school, he started noticing kids all around him staring. At first, Christian thought that maybe he looked funny or had something stuck in his shoes, so he just ignored it and kept walking towards his class. As he got closer to his class, he realized now kids were not only staring at him, but they were talking behind his back. It wasn't only like five students either. He noticed that almost everywhere he went, every single student he saw seemed to be talking about him.

"Will Christian please report to the principal's office," he heard over the loudspeakers.

"Great," he thought. "Thanks, all I needed was more attention."

When Christian arrived at the principal's office, she asked, "Christian, why did you do this?"

Confused, Christian asked, "Did what?"

"Stop playing dumb. We are having at least ten kids every thirty minutes coming in to tell us that you did it. Now tell me, why did you do it?"

With a sterner voice, Christian responded, "Maybe if you tell me, I will be able to know what I may have done."

With the principal looking closely at him, she said, "Christian, why did you completely graffiti your whole classroom?"

At first Christian fell for it. With all the intensity and all of the suspense that had just happened, he was almost convinced that he did do it. But eventually he got his head back, and said, "Um… I don't have the slightest clue what you are talking about. I never in my life have even touched a spray can, especially not just to go ruin a classroom."

The principal looked at him thoughtfully. "You don't seem like a kid who would do such things. Well, at least that's what your behavior and grades tell us. But either way, it's literally a hundred kids' voices versus yours. I can't do anything until either I find hard, solid proof that it wasn't you who graffitied the classroom, or all the kids who told me you're the guilty one take back their accusations. We will have a meeting with you and your parents at the end of the school day. Oh, and by the way, I suggest you find out who did it, because if you don't, you're expelled."

Christian walked out of the office with fear. He had no idea what to do, and even if he did have an idea of what to do, he had no idea how to even begin. He knew that it was going to be hard, but he couldn't be expelled. He knew he had eight hours to get all the information he needed. He knew that at this point his knowledge and his skills were going to come in handy today.

On the outside, Christian looked confident and ready to get down to business, but on the inside, he knew he was in grave danger. He didn't know where to start. He had zero clues of who would want to frame him. When nutrition came, he went to the library and sat down very stressed.

"Yo, Christian."

Christian looked up to see his two friends Charlie and Rosie. Charlie said, "We heard about what happened, and if there is anything we can do to help, just ask." Christian didn't care. He was just there looking down and worried about what would happen to him.

"It's okay, guys. It's not like we can do anything." As Christian's friends were heading off, he decided to leave the library and visit the class that was graffitied up. Of course, nobody was there, so he took the opportunity to look around for ten minutes. When he left, he heard someone say his name.

"Oh no, not this guy," he said to himself.

"Looks like you finally got what you deserved, idiot."

"Get lost, Robert. Nobody called you." Robert's goal was to make Christian's life as miserable as possible. Christian didn't know why Robert hated him. He just figured there was always that one kid who thought he was better than everyone else, and in this case it was Robert. Robert laughed and walked away.

Eventually, Christian bumped into his friends again. Rosie said, "Hey, we don't care if you don't want us to help. As much as we know you're smart, we both know you can't solve this on your own."

Christian replied, asking, "Well, what can you do?"

"That's exactly why we came."

She handed him a receipt that said, "Twelve spray cans for the total price of twenty dollars."

"You think these were the ones used to spray the classroom?"

"That's exactly what we think. We found the receipt on the floor of the graffitied classroom," replied Charlie.

"That's great and all, but this doesn't give us the person who sprayed the classroom."

"That's true, but look where it was purchased. A thrift shop, specifically the one around the corner. And we all know kids under the age of eighteen are not allowed in there."

"Whoa, you're trying to tell me it was an adult, like a teacher?" Both Charlie and Rosie nodded their heads. But why a teacher? Christian couldn't believe what had just happened, he just couldn't.

"I mean, think about it, Christian," Rosie said. "Mr. Fernandez hates you. He hates how you're literally always correcting him, how sometimes you take over the class and you make him sound dumb. He hates how you are always one step ahead of him, he hates how—"

Christian interrupted Rosie and said, "No, it can't be. That's just stupid."

Charlie quickly added, saying, "Is it? That would explain why there was no footage. Only a teacher would know how to disable the cameras."

Christian was convinced, but there was still the major problem of how they were going to be able to prove this to the principal.

"We can't just simply show her this receipt," he said.

Everyone stayed quiet for a moment as they saw Mr. Fernandez.

"I'm very disappointed, Christian," Mr. Fernandez said as he walked past them. "Top of the class student doing things like this is not good at all. You're getting what you deserve."

With that, Mr. Fernandez left. Christian was clenching his fist. His friends noticed as well, so Charlie said, "Dude, are you okay?"

Christian replied, "I'm fine. So, are we going to get me

cleared or what? I have seven hours to get my proof and catch Mr. Fernandez. Are you going to help?"

Smiling, Rosie and Charlie said yes with excitement.

"Well, how do we start, Christian?" asked Rosie.

Christian studied the receipt and said, "Well, we know that it says that the purchase was done at five p.m. exactly on Saturday, which means someone had to break into school and do it at a time when nobody was here. We know that at six the janitor comes to clean up and make sure that the school is properly closed, and Mr. Fernandez couldn't have sprayed the whole class and deleted the footage from the cameras in one hour."

Rosie responded, saying, "You think he had help?"

"I'm pretty sure he did," said Charlie.

"I just don't see him doing all this in an hour considering the class is pretty big. Plus, look at this. There were twelve bottles bought. That seems too much for just one person. I'm almost certain he had help."

"Who do you think helped him?" asked Charlie.

"I don't know, but that's not important right now. Right now, I want to do this—I want you two to follow Mr. Fernandez, even if it means ditching class."

"What about you, Christian? What are you going to do?"

asked Rosie.

"Well, to be honest, I'm not even supposed to be here. I'm supposed to be in the counseling office. But I have more important things to do. I'll be somewhere else. Just please do what I said."

With that, they went their separate ways.

Christian knew very well who helped out Mr. Fernandez. The way he had looked at him that morning was enough to give it away. They both had given him that evil look. It was fairly obvious who it was. Christian started a video on his phone. He didn't care about getting the face; he knew the voice would be enough.

"'Sup, Robert," he said, walking up to Robert sitting outside of a classroom.

"What do you want? Aren't you supposed to be in counselling?"

Luckily, Robert was very stupid, so Christian used that to his advantage.

"I am, but you see, I'm trying to get my name cleared. You see, I know that it wasn't me who sprayed the class. Do you have any idea who it was?"

Robert laughed and came so close to Christian that he could smell the disgusting breath of what he recently ate in the cafeteria.

"Listen, I knew it wouldn't take you long to find out it was me who sprayed the class and tried to frame you, but c'mon. Most kids are convinced it was you. How dumb were you to accidentally forget your gym clothes?"

"So that's how you convinced kids to think it was me who sprayed the whole class," Christian thought.

"The point is, soon you'll be outta school and everything will be much better without you." Robert got up and left with a smirk.

As Robert left, Christian reached into his pocket, took out his phone, and ended the video. "Yes, Robert, I may be dumb for leaving my gym clothes, but you're even dumber for telling me your whole plan. How stupid can some people get."

Christian saved the video and quickly went to go find Rosie and Charlie.

Christian looked everywhere for Charlie and Rosie, and after an hour he finally managed to find them. He showed them the video.

"No way, you actually caught him saying that?" asked Rosie and Charlie.

"Yup, every single word. The only bad thing is he said

nothing about Mr. Fernandez helping him. Say, talking about Mr. Fernandez, did you notice anything weird about him?"

Both Charlie and Rosie smiled at each other and handed Christian a tape. "Is this—"

"The tape Mr. Fernandez took in order for nobody to see it was him and Robert who sprayed the class? Yes."

Christian asked, "How do you know this is the tape?"

Charlie replied, saying, "We were following Mr. Fernandez when we saw that he was talking to Robert and told him to destroy the tape. We managed to take it away when Robert left his backpack to go and play football."

Christian hugged both of them and said, "Well, there is only one thing to do now."

They all rushed to the principal's office.

"Oh, Christian. I didn't expect to see you here. Have any good news?"

"Oh, I have excellent news," said Christian as he handed the principal all the evidence they had gathered.

Several minutes later, the loudspeaker announced over the school: "MAY I SEE MR FERNANDEZ AND ROBERT IN THE PRINCIPAL'S OFFICE IMMEDIATELY."

Mr. Fernandez was awaited by the school's police and was arrested, and Robert was greeted by his parents and an officer as well.

"Mr. Fernandez, I'm disappointed," said the principal. "I expected more from you."

Mr. Fernandez didn't say anything but gave a cold look as he was taken away by the cops. As for Robert, he was sobbing like a baby as he and his parents were escorted by the officer as well.

"What's going to happen to him?" asked Rosie.

"Oh, he will probably just face a minor punishment. Probably go to court, who knows." The principal looked at Christian and said, "Sorry for blaming all this on you."

"It's fine," said Christian.

"It's amazing, you're only sixteen and are smart enough to get yourself cleared in less than eight hours."

"Well, I had help," said Christian, looking at both Charlie and Rosie.

"You guys are going to go far. Trust me, you're all going to be successful in life."

As Christian, Rosie, and Charlie were going home, they were all smiling, having a nice, normal conversation.

"And you wanted to do this all by yourself," said Rosie, mocking Christian's voice.

Christian laughed.

Charlie added, "We all make a great team, don't we?"

As they arrived at Christian's house, he said, "Well, we do. I'll never doubt you again." They went inside the house, now knowing success comes in a team rather than in one mind who thinks he could do it all.

Michael Blancas

Run Boy Run
Jeffrey Carrasco

It was Thursday, November 16, 2017, two days before the Cross Country State Finals. Carlos was out with his girlfriend, Samantha, and his teammates. They had just finished their last practice before going to Fresno the next day to compete on Saturday. They each waited outside of school for their parents to pick them up. One by one, each person drove away, leaving Carlos and his long-time XC friend, Thomas. Carlos sauntered towards Thomas with a smile from ear to ear.

He laughed, "Dude! I can't believe we're going to State freaking Finals. Can you believe this?"

Thomas, equally eager, added, "I know! I've always wanted to go to State Finals before Junior year, and now knowing that we're going this Saturday is—"

Right before he could finish, his dad arrived honking like there was no tomorrow.

"Oh shoot, my dad's here. Well, I'll see you tomorrow!"

Carlos turned towards the car as Thomas ran to it, and shouted and shouted after him, "Don't forget, tomorrow at 12:15 sharp, here at school!"

Thomas left, and Carlos realized his parents weren't going to come for him. Carlos didn't mind. He always liked running home when his parents couldn't pick him up. After all, that is what he was good at.

Carlos was lying on his stomach when he woke up to the sound of his alarm. It rang specifically at 8:37 a.m. He jumped out of his bed and headed towards his drawer. He took out some black running shorts, and put on a shirt and some socks. All he needed were his training shoes, but he could not find them. Concerned, he started looking everywhere he thought he could have left them. As he was looking under his bed, his mom came in and whispered, "Are you looking for these?" In her hand were Carlos's training shoes dangling by the laces.

"Yeah, where'd you find them?"

"You left them outside last night and I brought them in this morning when I got home from work." There was a silence in the room. The only sound heard was the snoring of Carlos's little brother, Diego, and the constant moving of Valeria, Carlos's little sister.

Breaking the silence, Carlos's mom complained, "Why are these shoes so heavy?" As she spoke, he got up and took the shoes to put them on.

"They're my trainers, Ma. They're heavy because when I run in them I get used to the extra weight. Then when I wear my racing flats, I'm able to run faster and PR on my races."

"What in the world is PR? You and your alien terminology."

"It means personal record, Ma. Come on. I'll be back at 11:45 to get my things before I leave for tomorrow's race."

Carlos's mom stood in silence for a while, then finally spoke, "Why don't you come at 12:30?"

"I will be gone by then. Remember, I told you all about it last week?"

She stood trying to remember, knowing she hadn't been paying attention. "I thought your race was on Sunday."

At this point Carlos was frustrated. His mom was almost never at home because of work, and when she was, she was asleep or getting ready to go to work again. His father was in and out of the city due to his job, and he hadn't actually been home in two months. It was in that moment that Carlos wanted to scream and cry out to his mom, but he decided to continue walking towards the door.

He could feel a lump the size of a soccer ball lodged in his throat, and then he said, "You know what? Why do I even bother telling you anything? You never pay attention, and you're never home. I'm always taking care of Val and Diego. I'm always with them. I always have to cook for them. I already have enough stress with my homework and my classes, then I have to come home and be the parent in the house!" Before bawling out in front of his mom, and before she could say anything, he went on and started his long run.

Carlos knew that yelling at his mom wasn't the best way to cope and let out his emotions. He simply was tired of not having someone to be there for him in his good times and bad times. By then, it was 11:37, and Carlos was on his twenty-second mile. He had lost track of time, and still had to go home and shower to be at school by 12:15. He sprinted home, which was two miles from where he was at. As he turned the corner to get home, he slipped on a pile of dog waste and fell on his right ankle. He felt the pain rush through the tendons in his leg—peroneus longus, peroneus brevis. He lay on the ground until the tamale lady, Martha, ran up to him and asked if he was okay.

"Mijo, are you okay? You took a pretty big fall there."

"Yeah, yeah, my ankle hurts a little. Oh god."

Carlos knew that something wasn't right with his leg, but avoiding the worst, he told himself it was just the pain of the fall. Returning from his thoughts, he asked repeatedly for the time.

"Hey, miss, miss, what time is it?"

"The time? Forget about the time. We need to get you checked up."

"No, no, I'll be fine. Just please tell me the time!"

"Okay, okay, no need to yell, one moment." She realized that she couldn't leave Carlos alone, so she called her daughter to give her the time.

"Luuupppeeeee! Que hora es?"

"11:49!"

Hearing little Lupe say eleven forty-nine brought Carlos up to his feet. He forgot the pain. He forgot what had happned with his mom. All that filled his mind was getting home to get his things and getting to school before the bus left.

With sweat running down his forehead and down his chest, he arrived in front of the school parking lot. His coach Robert Russell and assistant coach Francesca Quíjada were waiting. Coach Rob turned and saw Carlos limping towards the bus.

"Carlos, you're five minutes late. What's wrong? Why are

you limping?"

"It's fine, Mr. Russell. I'm okay. I just ran a short tempo run, and I slipped on my way here. But I'm okay, I swear!"

"You don't look so good. How do you feel? Does anything hurt?"

"Yeah, Mr. Russell. I'm fine, just need to rest up for to-morrow."

"Alright, then get in. We're going to be late. Make sure to remind me to check it out later."

With this, Carlos was now on his way to the CIF XC State Finals. Joy and comfort filled his heart and mind. Being with his friends was like being with a family that was always there for him, who would always be by his side through thick and thin. On their way to Fresno, Carlos was telling his team-mates about his ankle injury.

"Yo, my ankle really hurts. I fell and ate crap in front of the tamale lady. She straight up was about to call an ambu-lance."

Eagerly and worriedly, his teammates got closer to listen. Some even asked if he was able to run.

"Dude, this isn't good."

"Where does it hurt?"

"How bad did you eat it?"

Worrying that Mr. Russell would hear, he anxiously told them to be quiet and to talk about a different subject.

Shaken by a bump in the parking lot of a hotel, Carlos woke up to the realization that he had arrived in Fresno. He heard his friends talking about how they'd PR, and how they'd hope to win State. As they were about to get off the bus, Carlos began to feel intense sharp pain in his ankle. He fell to the ground and could not get up. His friends Thomas and Ethan helped him up and asked if he was okay.

"Yo, you good, bro?"

"Yeah, it's just this stupid ankle. I guess I'm going to have to use the R.I.C.E. method." R.I.C.E. stood for rest, ice, compression, and elevation. Carlos hoped it would be enough to get him ready to run.

"Dang, don't let Russell find out, or you won't be able to run tomorrow at all."

This was the last thing Carlos wanted, to not be included in the State Final race against the top schools in the league. He was thinking about how Mr. Russell would react to finding out that he lied to him, and how he never told him that he was injured. Carlos began to stress about what the whole team back in L.A. would say, how he let them down. So much stress built up in him. He began to stress about his family, how he shouted at his mother, how bad he must have made her feel after he left her. How he was being rude to Martha the tamale lady who was only trying to help him. Carlos felt as if his whole world was collapsing. He wanted to be left alone and unheard of. He knew that if he told Russell that he was hurt, he would not let him run the next day. With all the stress in his mind, Carlos took a long warm shower and R.I.C.E.'d his knee before he went to sleep.

"Wake up, princess," shouted Thomas from the bed across the room.

"Hurry up, you have twenty minutes to get ready. Coach wants us out by 6:00."

"Bro, what time is it? Oh crap, is it already Saturday?"

"Yes, now get up before he gets upset."

Carlos got up, went to go wash his face, comb his hair, and was in the middle of putting on his jeans when he re-alized he didn't have any pain in his ankle. He was not sure if it was because he had just woken up and his body wasn't reminded that he was injured, or if he was overreacting to his fall the day prior. Either way, Carlos felt good, and his con-fidence went up. He was no longer worried about not being able to run the meet. After changing, they were off to go eat breakfast at a local restaurant. Then they went to Woodward Park where the State Finals would be held.

Upon their arrival, Carlos and his teammates went to go check out the course before they ran. Each were very nervous, and some a bit overwhelmed.

"Duuude, we're actually here. Like, what the actual heck."

"I don't know if I can run this, dude. Look at Justin Brown's time. We won't beat that!"

"Relax, foo, everything will come out good."

As they all expressed how they felt, Carlos slowed down to watch the ducks in the pond. His good old friend Thomas was there next to him.

"Dude, I'm worried about my ankle. I don't know if it's fully healed."

"Maybe it was something small, nothing serious. You did say you didn't feel any pain, right?"

"Yeah, but still, it hurt all day yesterday and now I don't feel anything? Something can't be right. Who knows, maybe I'm ju—"

Just as he was about to finish, the call for his race was announced: "Division Two Boys Race in ten minutes!"

"Oh shoot, let's go. That's our call!"

"Bravo, Downtown Magnet, Eagle Rock, Franklin, Imperial High, Legacy, Lincoln, Marquez, Marshall, Mendez, Santee, Torres, Wilson at your positions!" called the announcer. The race was going to begin in two minutes. Before they started, coach Russell gave the team a few words of advice.

"Look, I know it took us a lot of hard work, determination, time, and commitment to get here, but we made it to State Finals! Be proud of yourselves. Look at what you have accomplished. You guys reached the goal of getting here. Now, whether you win or lose, just know that you have a whole team in L.A. and coaches who are proud of your accomplishments. Now, remember to *PUSH* your way through this race. Can someone tell me what I mean by that?"

"Persist Until Success Happens!"

"Thank you to whichever one of you who said that. Now, let's go out there and show the others who the champs are."

"On your mark… get set…" followed by a gun shot. The runners began their run. In the lead was Eagle Rock, followed by Franklin, then Bravo. In the Bravo team lead, Thomas followed by Carlos and other teammates. When they reached the mile mark, the time was at 4:47. At this point, Carlos was in third place. He remained in third place until before the second mile where the hills were. Since Carlos lived near Ascot Hills, a running course in L.A. which had lots of hills, he had no trouble going up the inclines. He was now in first place. The hills only lasted for about a quarter of a mile. Going downhill was the tricky part. Carlos knew that to stay in first place he had to go down the hill fast but carefully. With no time to think, he sprinted down the hill as if some monster from a horror movie was chasing him. Carlos immediately felt a crack in his ankle. He felt no pain, but he definitely knew something was wrong. He was about half a mile away from the finish line and was about fifty to fifty-five yards ahead of the other teams. As he was running, he suddenly felt the sharp pain he did not want to feel from the beginning of the race. He knew sooner or later he was going to collapse. Turning and seeing the other teams get closer and closer, the step did not help Carlos's state of mind. He was nervous, and was about to have a panic attack.

His inner conscience began to talk to him: *You're such an idiot! You never should have ran yesterday morning. This wouldn't be happening if you weren't such a try-hard! What an idiot.*

He began hearing the voice of his coach in his head: *Your legs are not giving out. Your head is giving up. KEEP GOING! Your body can stand anything; it's your mind you have to con-*

vince.

Then he began to hear his mother, words she had said long ago when he was a child: *Mijo, I wish you the strength to face challenges with confidence. Choose your battles carefully, and take risks carefully. Remember how much you are loved!*

With all of these voices, Carlos thought maybe he had schizophrenia. He laughed and tried to run, but as he made the next step, he fell to his knees. He knew that this was the end, the end of his cross country career, the end of his world. But then he remembered the things he heard his coach and mom say. He told himself that he would not quit easily. He got back up and ran as fast as he could. The other runners were getting closer. Each step he took only brought more pain to his ankle. As he reached the final forty meters, he saw people cheering from the left and right side with posters, and people leaning over the railing to cheer him on as he finished the race. In front of him, only a few meters away he saw that golden yellow ribbon across the course waiting for him to pass through it. Just as he was a few feet away, he saw two people both from opposite teams pass him and cross the finish line in front of his eyes. Carlos then went on to cross the line third and collapsed right after. He was covered in sweat and tears. Carlos did not care if he did not finish first. All that mattered to him was that he finished the race and tried his absolute best. After being carried to the clinic that was posted for the race, to Carlos's surprise, he saw his mother, father, Diego and Valeria. His mother ran towards him to give him a hug. At that moment, Carlos began to cry. Just as she did, he tried to communicate with her, but the words would not come out.

"I...I...I love...love you, m-m-mom. I'm sorry for screaming at you. I didn't mean to hurt your feelings."

"Aw, it's ok sweetie. I know you were just upset, and you didn't mean it. It happens to all of us. Don't worry. Come on, let's go outside."

Leaning against his mom and limping out of the clinic doors, Carlos looked at his dad and they both smiled. As he put on his Bravo cap, he saw his teammates, Coach Russell, Assistant Coach Francesca Quíjada, all of the other teams that competed, and the families of those who ran. They all applauded him and chanted his name. Each person congratulated him on finishing the race. Tears covered Carlos's face. All he could say was, "Thank you!"

Soon after, the award ceremony had begun, and Carlos, along with runners from Eagle Rock and from Marshall, stood on the first, second, and third platforms. Eagle Rock had won first, Marshall second, and Bravo third. The competitors brought up Carlos to the first place stand and applauded him one last time.

Alas, as everybody left the park, the team gathered for pictures and food, each congratulating one another and telling their own experience. Thomas and Carlos began to talk about how their race went and how they felt.

"Yo, Carlos, what you did was absolutely badass. I wouldn't have kept on running."

"Dude, I know. Honest to God, I was going to stop, but something kept me going."

"Man, I still don't know how you did it, but that was pretty sick. I saw your parents at the end of the race. They were looking for you."

"Yeah, I know. I saw them at the clinic. They're taking me back home because they want to go to the hospital to check if there's anything serious."

"Dang, does it hurt?"

"Now only a little. They gave me some Motrin to relieve the pain. I told my mom I'd be lying down in the back seat so I can get some rest."

"Oh, wait, is it that green truck over there?"

"Over where?"

As he turns, he sees his family drive out of the parking lot.

"Oh crap, they probably think I'm in the back seat. Bye! I'll see you later!"

As Carlos hops away, Thomas yells out three unforgettable words: "Run, boy, run!"

Everybody is a champion, win or lose, The reward for success is the opportunity to do more. Effort only fully releases its reward after a person refuses to quit. From here on out, you go all the way up. It begins now.

Jeffrey Carrasco

The Finishing Line
Emely Toscano

I woke up to my older sister getting ready and doing her makeup. My bed covers smelled like the waffles and fresh strawberries that my mom would make for me twelve years ago when I was five. After I finished eating, my mom gave me a huge hug and told me, "I love you, Alissa." As I was walking to school, I thought of how lucky I was to have my amazing parents healthy and alive, and how other kids weren't lucky enough to have their parents. My day at school was amazing. I scored an A on the math test that would count the most towards next year when I begin college. My classmates were troublemakers. As I looked around, I saw many Fs on my classmates' papers. In the back, I heard one kid saying, "F for fantastic."

"Haha," my other classmates giggled.

I came home to a huge surprise for my father celebrating his forty-fifth birthday. We had cake, shared our favorite memories, and drank hot chocolate by our fireplace in the backyard. As I was falling asleep, my sister and I talked about how amazing our parents were and all the sacrifices they did just to make us happy. As I slept, I dreamt my worst nightmare, that my father had passed away. It's not that I just love my father, but he's the one who works to maintain my family. My whole face was wet when I woke up.

The next day I was at school taking notes. Suddenly I heard my phone buzzing and saw eighteen missed calls from my mom.

"Um…excuse me, Mr. P, can I go to the restroom?" I asked.

Before I answered the phone, I wondered what could possibly be wrong. As soon as I answered, I heard my mom desperately crying as if she was in some serious pain.

"Mom, what's wrong?" I asked.

Slowly she began, word by word, saying, "Your father—" stopping mid-sentence to catch her breath. I heard a hard swallow, and then, "He…he's gone."

In that moment, I felt like my heart was being crushed into pieces. I could feel warm tears rushing down my face, and the only thing that popped in my mind was running out of school and going straight to the hospital. Ten minutes later, my sister picked me up, and we drove right to the hospital. As soon as I saw his body lying on the bed, I rushed to his side. With my arms draped around him, I watched as my tears hit his body like nails being driven into a wooden coffin. Suddenly, I got a flashback to when I was eight years old, when my dad would take me out to Sammy's for ice cream. I remembered the exact words as if they were printed onto my heart as he was holding my soft, moisturized hands.

"My love, you have to finish college and give your own kids a better life," he said.

"Why, why, why?" I screamed as I came back to my hard reality. I said to myself, What are we going to do now?

I knew things in my house weren't going to be the same. Of course, my mom was going to have to hustle harder. I would never manage to have a smile on my face from that point on.

The next time I went to class, all I was able to do was take out a notebook and start drawing random stuff without paying attention to what it was. Deep in my imagination, I pictured myself at the park holding cotton candy, laughing at his jokes and riding our bikes together. My eyes got extremely watery.

In the distance I heard my teaching asking me, "Alissa? Is

everything alright?"

"Yeah," I said, hiding my attitude.

My father would always tell me to be a strong girl just like my older sister. I was totally subdued by the fact that my mom and my older sister were going to have to struggle and work very hard. When I got home, my mom was sitting down in the living room with my two sisters. By that time, I knew there were going to be drastic changes in my life.

"You, your sister, and I are going to apply for jobs, because we're not going to be able to pay all the bills."

That was fine with me. I wasn't going to argue with my mom, because I knew the type of situation we were in. I didn't want to rebel against her. As I was falling asleep, my older sister and I were having a conversation about how she was still going to continue with college and how I was still going to continue with my last year of high school. I knew life wasn't going to be easy, but my father's words were constantly running through my mind like little kids running back and forth, telling me I had to subsist.

The next day I skipped school. My sister and I went out to look for work. Finally, after five hours of searching and searching, we found jobs. We were going to work at the ice cream place my dad got his first job at. I was kind of motivated, because my dad had known the owner, and they were good friends. So, I was pretty confident, and I was really excited about what was going to come next. My sister and I were met with a bad surprise when we got home. My mom had broken her arm, and she couldn't go to work.

"I am so sorry this happened," she said to my sister and me.

"It's okay, Mom," we said.

As soon as I got to my room, I threw myself in bed and sighed. I thought of how bad my life was right now, and how much I wished my dad was here. But I couldn't complain. The only thing I could do was just keep my head up and not let the bad situations bring me down. The next day, I went to school and got my test results back. I scored an A on one of my big tests. A huge smile appeared on my face. After school, I went to work. I felt very confident with Susan, the lady who owned the ice cream shop.

As I was working, she said, "You seem like a very hard working young lady."

"Yes, I need to work hard for my mom." Later on, I opened myself up to her. I told her that I wanted to make my mom really proud of me, and make my dad proud as well, even if he wasn't here. I told her I wanted to graduate college and be a successful girl. My sister and I had so much fun. Susan was really nice. She let my sister and I keep the tips we earned that day. My first day was great. I went home and shared the great experience with my mom and my younger sister.

It seemed like every other day of my life was just getting worse and worse though. My sister got severely sick. And we had to pay the rent in just five days, though we only had 400 dollars. I went to school, and right after took the Dash to work. I entered a little late, but when I explained to Susan what had happened, she understood me.

I told her about the rent situation, and she said, "I'll lend you the money you need. You seem like you really care about your family, and I want to help you achieve that."

I gave her a huge hug and said, "Thank you. Thank you, Susan."

I came home to tell my mom and my sisters the great news. They were so happy, and my mom called Susan to tell her thank you.

We paid the rent, and everything was fine. But I had received a letter from school saying that I needed to get my grades from a C to an A. I was definitely tired from work and school, and now I had to study even more. That night I went to sleep at three in the morning.

The next day I had to go to school and go to work. At school we were getting ready for the SAT. I had to study really hard, but I knew that if I scored well, then I'd get accepted to many universities and be very successful in life.

The next day, I had to make the hardest decision of my life—either go to my best friend's party or study. My best friend had always been there for me, especially when my father passed. I decided to study, because I knew that my whole life depended that choice. If I did well on the test, I would have a great future. My best friend got mad at me, but I told her if she really was my best friend, then she would really understand and respect my decision.

The next day, I asked her, "Are you mad?"

"I understand you're in a really hard situation," she said, "but this was my big party, and you missed out."

"I know. I'm truly sorry. I had to study for my test."

"It's okay," she said, giving me a big hug.

I did well on the test after all, and later got accepted to the greatest university of all time. I knew this would be the door to great opportunities and having a better future.

Before starting college, I had been really stressed. I had been getting annoyed by my mom, the bills we had to pay, school, the emails I was receiving from my teachers, and my job. My only motivation was my father's death. I was sad, but I knew that I had done something positive, and that I was going to be successful in life. My mom, my sister, and I had already gotten settled. My mom started working again, and we weren't struggling economically.

I started my first year of college, and I was passing all my classes with As. My new journey had just started. I had gotten through all the ups and downs. My mom and my sisters were happy, and I knew that if my dad were here, he would be proud of me as well.

After running all my errands one day, I finally stopped by the cemetery and sat next to my dad's tombstone. Happily, I said, "Dad, I made it."

Emely Toscano

Time Will Tell
Janette Lopez
PART I

It is 6:50 in the morning, February 2017. I pull myself out of bed, make my way over to my window, and stare at the grayish, blueish, greenish and white apartments blocking my view. There's something about the blue sky that feels safe and peaceful. I remember last year I would waste five, sometimes ten minutes looking up at the sky. Why the hell do I have to go to school? I think to myself. I look over to my sister's side of the bed. Her alarm clock is buzzing like a five-year old who's drank ten frappuccinos. It's 7:00 am now. I hit the alarm.

"Get up, fatty! Sadly, it's time for school."

"I'm up, I'm up," my sister says, still groggy. I quickly put on my clothes, fix the bed, and run downstairs to the restroom. I straighten my hair, brush my teeth, and by the time I'm done, it's 7:40 a.m. Damn. No time to eat.

As I walk out the gate to go to school with my brother, I see my homegirl waiting for me. I remember we had planned to go to Starbucks. After getting my Starbucks, we walk to school. As I walk into class, everyone turns to see who walked in. I approach my seat, and my teacher calls me over.

"I can see why you're always late," she says.

"I suppose it doesn't have to concern you," I say.

"Look, Lexi, you're right it doesn't have to concern me, but I know you're a great student. I know you can succeed and be someone in life. You just don't want to."

I walk out of her class to the restroom. As I walk, I think, damn, why is she right?

The bell rings. It's break. I meet up with my friends, we have our fun, and next thing you know it's time to go to third period. I haven't been to school for a while, so I didn't know we had a quiz. I try my best, although I don't know anything. The forty-one minutes of class pass by quickly. As I walk towards my fourth period class, as usual, my teacher opens the door. I walk in, and he greets us.

"Good afternoon," he says as I walk to my seat.

I do my work and learn something. It is hard, but I do it. After finishing the last problem on my paper, I pack up and the bell rings. Lunch comes, and I walk down with my homegirl.

The day goes by quickly. As I walk to my last class, I see him—Andy Castro. He is the cutest eleventh grader on the planet, at least in my mind. I remember our first and only conversation. It was sixth period, and he was wearing his basketball jersey. I'm sure he has no idea I even exist. But anyways, I have to continue walking as I'm entering my homegirl's class. I decide to stay there.

As she is doing her work, I think to myself how good my day has been. I look at the clock. It is 1:30, three minutes before the bell will ring. Those three minutes go by quickly, and as soon as I hear the bell, I leave the classroom.

I make my way to the bike rack to meet up. Tyler and all these annoying kids are rushing their way out the gate and to the metro station. It is so loud I barely hear my brother when he says, "You ready? Let's go." We make our way home.

When we walk in, no one is there. I quickly scan our kitchen table. Nothing but bills, old newspapers, and neatly cut coupons in one pile. A few minutes later, my mom walks in.

"I tried calling you after school and you didn't answer. Why?" she asks with an obvious attitude, as she folds her arms.

"Oh...I forgot my phone was on mute, and I didn't check it until now," I answer, purposely avoiding eye contact with her.

"Well," she says, shifting her body weight from one foot to the other, "I found out that you have been missing school a lot, and I want you to tell me why! Where have you been going?" She demands, yanking my earbuds out of my ears.

Think, think, I tell myself.

I guess her maternal instinct to lecture reaches its boiling point. "I'm always going to tell you the same thing over and over no matter how much you hate me. You have to understand we do this for your own good, and I'm having a serious conversation right now." She pauses briefly, grabbing the bottom of my chin with her hand. "Look at me. I don't want you missing school anymore." She starts walking towards the kitchen table, but suddenly she looks over her shoulder and says, "To be honest with you, sometimes I don't think you're going to graduate."

Before I know it, we are arguing.

"MOM," I say, with a little bit more force than I intend. "I love you and all, but do you ever think that you're the reason why I'm doing bad in school?" I ask her. Almost instantly, shock spreads across her face like a California wildfire. I continue, refusing to let my tears be seen. "You always make these comments and never think to ask yourself how they make me feel?" Suddenly, I can't help it. I am powerless as my warm tears bully their way down my cheeks. "But you know what, I'm going to prove you wrong. And when I'm graduating, I don't want to see you there," I scream before running to my room.

After I slam my door, I hear her shout back, "Well, whether you like it or not, I'm going to be there."

PART II

It has been a year, and to my own surprise, I've made it. I'm a part of the graduating class of 2018. I look at my sixth period soccer class and the thirty students in white shirts and black shorts running up and down the soccer field. Then I hear, "Lexi, why aren't you on the field?" Our P.E. teacher is shouting across the field. "Hurry up. Takes teamwork to make the dream work," he says.

That's funny, it's the same thing the school therapist says after our weekly check-in sessions. As I start jogging over to the field, I flash back on the last year of my life: Me staying after school with my tutor. Me crying in the principal's office. Me catching three buses to study at the Barnes and Noble in Long Beach. Me not speaking to my mom for the last year.

After school, I walk home alone, since my brother graduated last year. I shove my earphones in my ears and start walking. While I'm waiting for the light to change, I check my phone and see I have twenty missed calls from my dad. I try calling back, but there is no answer, so I rush the rest of the way home. When I walk in, my dad isn't there. My siblings are sitting in the old brown couch, my younger sister watching TV and my brother as worried as I am, having also missed calls from my dad.

A few hours later, my dad walks in looking down and sad. My brother and I quickly look up at him, but all he does is say, "Kids, sit down."

I get a feeling in my guts that something wrong is about to go on. He turns off the TV and takes two steps forward, then he says that he needs to tell us something serious. Before he says another word, I interrupt and ask where mom is.

He says, "That's what I need to talk to you guys about, mija."

"What happened?!" we ask.

"I'm sorry kids but...your mother isn't with us anymore. She got in a car accident and didn't make it."

My dad is trying to resist his tears, but he can't and starts crying.

"What? No, you're lying, dad. It can't be. How? Why her? Not MOM!"

We all burst into tears. My heart is breaking. I think

about how we got into that argument a year ago, and how we haven't talked ever since.

"Everything's my fault. I didn't even get to say goodbye," I say, as we all get up to hug him.

"No, it's not," Tyler says.

I run to my room. All I can think about is when I told my mom I didn't want to see her at my graduation. I was heartless. I miss my mom. Part of me is relieved, because at least she passed away knowing I was finally doing well.

As the days pass, I don't feel like me. I am completely lost, unable to express what has just happened and refusing to allow the process of healing to begin by closing myself off from everyone around me. I know my siblings and dad are going through the same situation, but I am still closing myself off. The holidays aren't going to be the same anymore. Her funeral is the worst part. Saying goodbye is hard because I haven't talked to my mom for a year. I remember how sometimes, when I would come home from school to find her in the kitchen with her white apron on, cooking her best food, she would see me walk in and say, "Hi, mija. How did it go in school today?" But I would just ignore her and walk past, straight to my room. Remembering her sad face because I wouldn't answer her makes me even more sad.

After the funeral, through the rest of January, I stop going to school.

In February, I wake up as usual, staring out my window up at the sky. This is how I have been wasting my time thinking about my mom. But today will be different.

My sister's alarm rings. It surprises me. I push my sister off the bed. She gets up scared, and says, "What is your problem?"

"I'm sorry. I'm just trying to cheer this family up again. It's time for school."

As I finish getting ready, I walk out the door. "Bye, fatty. I love you." I tell my sister for the first time.

I enter school and see Andy approaching me with my homegirl. She gives me a hug, and Andy awkwardly says, "Are you okay? Luci told me what happened with your mom. I'm sorry to hear that."

"Yeah, I guess I'm okay. Thanks for asking," I say. My homegirl pulls me to the side and tells Andy to give us a minute.

"He started talking to me last month when he saw you weren't coming to school anymore, and he was asking for you," my homegirl says.

"Oh, umm…" I say.

"'Oh, umm?' That's all you gotta say? Girl, I know you're going through a tough situation, but that doesn't have to stop you from enjoying your life."

I realize how right she is. "Okay, you're right," I tell her. As soon as I finish my sentence, the bell rings. Andy approaches us and says, "Let me walk with you to class."

"Umm…I lowkey forgot my classes," I say with a small laugh. "Let me go ask the office."

I walk into the office. On my left, all the ladies are on their computers and busy with school stuff. To my right there are empty black chairs. I make my way to the desk and ask for my classes. They print them out and give them to me. When I walk out, I see Andy still waiting for me.

"Let me see your classes." He takes a quick scan and says, "We have first through fourth and sixth together, so can I walk with you to class."

With a surprising and sad face I look up at him and tell him sure why not. As we're walking to class. There's nothing but silence for five minutes, then he starts a conversation.

"I have been through this situation. It's really hard to go through. It's hard to take in."

"Yes, it's hard," I say, but inside I'm thinking, You don't

know me. "Why?" I ask.

"Why what?"

"Why are you all of a sudden talking to me? I mean, there was last year, and until now?"

"Ever since that first conversation we had, I've been wanting to talk to you. But you would never go to six period, and I wouldn't see you around school that much. I thought you were busy catching up or something. And, well, I guess I finally grew the strength to come up to you to talk."

"Ohhh…okay," I say as we walk into class.

Before I know it, I'm rushing my way to sixth period. As I approach my locker to dress, Luci sees me and says, "Our coach isn't here, so it's a free period."

We walk into the gym, and the first person we see is Andy coming out of the boys' locker room with his basketball jersey on. He spots us out and sits in the white bleachers next to us.

"We haven't finished our conversation," he says. "I just wanted to say, keep your head up, and always remember to be you. Because after all, your mom is always watching you, and she's always going to want the best for you. Plus, she's always with you no matter where she's at." When he's done saying that, he leaves to practice.

The bell rings. The fifty-nine minutes of class have gone by quickly. I stay thinking about what Andy told me.

It is the end of February. Without realizing it, I've been slacking off again. But becoming best friends with Andy and talking with him for the past month has been the best. Andy has made me realize I have to choose between letting the death of my mother bring me down—and fail her—or if I am going to be Lexi and make my family proud of me—and graduate. Losing my mom is still hard for me, but I want to graduate to make my parents proud, I tell myself. I make my way to third period, walk in, open the laptop, log in, and check my grades. Because I've been slacking off, I have Fs again.

After school at home, it sounds so quiet without my mom. My dad walks in, all tired from work. "Hey, you're good?" he asks, sadly and tiredly.

"Yeah, I guess so," I say.

"Lexi, you have to get back on track. It's been months since your mom hasn't been with us. You have to move on and try your best. Keep your head up, mija."

"I am, Dad. Starting tomorrow, you're gonna have old Lexi back again."

"I love you, mija."

"I love you too, Dad," I say as I give him a hug.

My alarm wakes me up at seven the next morning as always. This day is different, though. I get ready, and as soon as I walk downstairs, my dad is waiting for me.

"Good morning, mija," he says.

"Good morning, Dad. Aren't you supposed to be at work?" I ask him with a surprised face.

"Yes, but I wanted to take you girls to school today. Where's your sister?"

"She's sick, so I told her to stay in bed. It's okay, I'll go walking. Dad, you rest and take care of my sister. Bye, Dad. I love you."

"Okay, pues, take care and do your best, because there's only a few months until graduation, and I want you to pick up those grades."

"Okay, Dad," I say as I'm out the door.

I leave early to school to ask all my teachers how I can catch up. They all help me. I have my tutor back again. Everyone is by my side, and their motivation is great. Though I miss my mom, I have to move on. I am back again. I still hurt, but realize that if I don't move on, I will only slack off more.

***

I can't believe it myself. The day has come. I am in my gold, sparkly dress with the blue gown on top. "Graduation day," I tell myself. I look all over the room for my family, but I don't see anyone. I see everyone else's families holding graduation balloons and flowers. I say, "Oh mom, where's my dad at?" I hear a voice as if it's coming from my head, calling my name. I turn and look around the court. I see my family. I give them hugs and tell myself, "Mom is really proud of me, and so am I. But where are you mom?"

Janette Lopez

Made in the USA
San Bernardino, CA
14 June 2018